**For my grandmother
Kathleen Llewellyn Montague,
who tends a year round garden**

VIKING
Published by Penguin Group
Penguin Young Readers Group, 345 Hudson Street, New York, New York 10014, U.S.A.

First published in 2003 by Viking, a division of Penguin Young Readers Group

3 5 7 9 10 8 6 4 2

LIBRARY OF CONGRESS CATALOGING-IN-PUBLICATION DATA
Cash, Megan Montague.
What makes the seasons? / by Megan Montague Cash.
p.   cm.
Summary: Easy rhyming text describes how plants grow and respond to seasonal changes.
ISBN 0-670-03598-X (hardcover)
1. Growth (Plants)—Juvenile literature. 2. Seasons—Juvenile literature.
[1. Growth (Plants) 2. Seasons.] I. Title.
QK731.C36 2003   571.8'2–dc21   2003001380

Manufactured in China
Set in Futura, Triplex
Book design by Teresa Kietlinski and Megan Montague Cash

What Makes the Seasons?

Megan Montague Cash

VIKING

The day began
with sprinkling rain
tapping at the windowpane.

Rain has turned the sky to gray.
Our snowman friend has gone away.

Fresh green leaves are peeking out.
What makes this their time to sprout?

Spring's mild weather
wakes the seeds,
bringing showers each seed needs.

Spring was here but couldn't stay.
Spring left on a **summer** day.
Plants that once were hardly there
now have flowers everywhere.

Each tree and weed and lima bean
shows its favorite shade of green.

Why is this a growing season?

Plants grow **tall**,

but what's the **reason**?

Plants grow best

in summer light,

when days are
long and **warm** and **bright**.

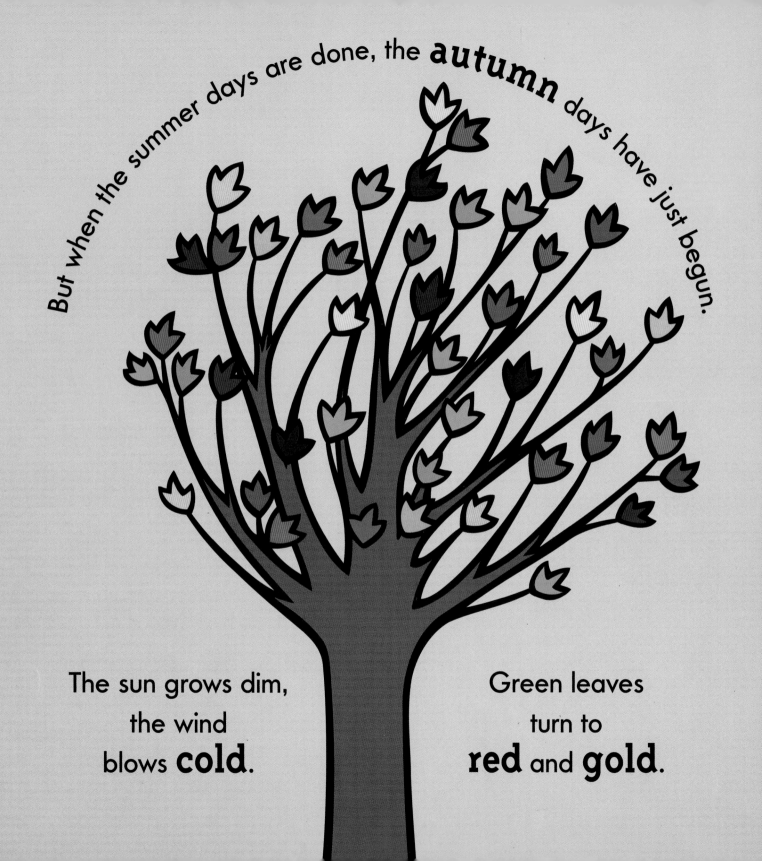

But when the summer days are done, the **autumn** days have just begun.

The sun grows dim, the wind blows **cold**.

Green leaves turn to **red** and **gold**.

The colored leaves **dance** all around.

In all the leaves on all the trees
are teeny tree food factories.

Leaves use sun to make the food.
When there's less sun, leaves come unglued.

The weather brought a change last night.
Winter turned the world to white.

Puffy flakes swirled high and low.

Snow makes flurries.
WHAT
makes snow?

In chilly clouds the raindrops **freeze**.

It's one of winter's **recipes**.

Winter is a time for sleep.
Trees are resting, seeds will keep.

Many creatures sleep and wait.
Winter's time to **hibernate**.

But what controls the season's change?
And what makes weather rearrange?

Earth's yearly trip around the sun

affects the seasons one by one.

In summer when the days are long
the sun shines down both hot and strong.

While winter has the shortest days—
less time for earth to get warm rays.

But when you have a winter day,
it's summer half the world away.

If summer blossoms open wide,
it's winter on earth's other side.

Seasons change
four times a year.
When each one ends,
the next one's here.

Enjoying changes
one by one
makes the seasons
so much fun.